The Adventures of PETER COTTONTAIL

Peter watched him go, until he was just a speck in the blue, blue sky

The Adventures of

PETER COTTONTAIL

by Thornton W. Burgess

illustrated by Harrison Cady

tempo books

GROSSET & DUNLAP
A FILMWAYS COMPANY
Publishers • New York

ISBN: 0-448-12754-7

Published by arrangement with Little, Brown and Company
Tempo Books is registered in the U.S. Patent Office
Printed in the United States of America

Contents

CONTENTS

Illustrations

ILLUSTRATIONS

I

Peter Rabbit Decides To Change His Name

PETER RABBIT! Peter Rabbit! I don't see what Mother Nature ever gave me such a common-sounding name as that for. People laugh at me, but if I had a fine-sounding name they wouldn't laugh. Some folks say that a name doesn't amount to anything, but it does. If I should do some wonderful thing, nobody would think anything of it.

No, Sir, nobody would think any-thing of it at all just because—why, just because it was done by Peter Rabbit."

Peter was talking out loud, but he was talking to himself. He sat in the dear Old Briar-patch with an ugly scowl on his usually happy face. The sun was shining, the Merry Little Breezes of Old Mother West Wind were dancing over the Green Meadows, the birds were singing, and happi-ness, the glad, joyous happiness of springtime, was everywhere but in Peter Rabbit's heart. There, there seemed to be no room for anything but discontent.

And such foolish discontent — discontent with his name! And yet, do you know, there are lots of people just as foolish as Peter Rabbit.

"Well, what are you going to do about it?"

The voice made Peter Rabbit jump and turn around hastily. There was Jimmy Skunk poking his head in at the opening of one of Peter's private little paths. He was grinning, and Peter knew by that grin that Jimmy had heard what he had said. Peter didn't know what to say. He hung his head in a very shame-faced way.

[*13*]

"You've got something to learn," said Jimmy Skunk.

"What is it?" asked Peter.

"It's just this," replied Jimmy.

> "There's nothing in a name except
>   Just what we choose to make it.
> It lies with us and no one else
>   How other folks shall take it.
> It's what we do and what we say
> And how we live each passing day
> That makes it big or makes it small
> Or even worse than none at all.
> A name just stands for what we are;
>   It's what we choose to make it.
> And that's the way and only way
>   That other folks will take it."

Peter Rabbit made a face at Jimmy Skunk. "I don't like being preached to."

"I'm not preaching; I'm just

[14]

telling you what you ought to know without being told," replied Jimmy Skunk. "If you don't like your name, why don't you change it?"

"What's that?" cried Peter sharply.

"If you don't like your name, why don't you change it?" repeated Jimmy.

Peter sat up and the disagreeable frown had left his face. "I—I—hadn't thought of that," he said slowly. "Do you suppose I could, Jimmy Skunk?"

"Easiest thing in the world," replied Jimmy Skunk. "Just decide what name you like and

[15]

then ask all your friends to call you by it."

"I believe I will!" cried Peter Rabbit.

"Well, let me know what it is when you have decided," said Jimmy, as he started for home. And all the way up the Crooked Little Path, Jimmy chuckled to himself as he thought of foolish Peter Rabbit trying to change his name.

II

Peter Finds a Name

PETER RABBIT had quite lost his appetite. When Peter forgets to eat, you may make up your mind that Peter has something very important to think about. At least, he has something on his mind that he thinks is important. The fact is, Peter had fully made up his mind to change his name. He thought Peter Rabbit too common a name. But when he tried to think of a better one, he found that no name that he could think of really pleased him any more. So he thought and he thought and he thought and he thought. And the more he thought the less appetite he had.

Now Jimmy Skunk was the only one to whom Peter had told how discontented he was with his name, and it was Jimmy who had suggested to Peter that he change it. Jimmy thought it a great joke, and he straightway passed the word along among all the little meadow and forest people that Peter Rabbit was going to change

[18]

his name. Everybody laughed and chuckled over the thought of Peter Rabbit's foolishness, and they planned to have a great deal of fun with Peter as soon as he should tell them his new name.

Peter was sitting on the edge of the Old Briar-patch one morning when Ol' Mistah Buzzard passed, flying low. "Good mo'ning, Brer Cottontail," said Ol' Mistah Buzzard, with a twinkle in his eye.

At first Peter didn't understand that Ol' Mistah Buzzard was speaking to him, and by the time he did it was too late to reply, for Ol' Mistah Buzzard was way,

way up in the blue, blue sky.

"Cottontail, Cottontail," said Peter over and over to himself and began to smile. Every time he said it he liked it better.

"Cottontail, Peter Cottontail! How much better sounding that is than Peter Rabbit! That sounds as if I really were somebody. Yes, Sir, that's the very name I want. Now I must send word to all my friends that hereafter I am no longer Peter Rabbit, but Peter Cottontail."

Peter kicked up his heels in just the funny way he always does when he is pleased. Suddenly he remembered that such a fine,

"Cottontail, Cottontail," said Peter over
and over to himself

long, high-sounding name as Peter
Cottontail demanded dignity. So
he stopped kicking up his heels
and began to practice putting on
airs. But first he called to the
Merry Little Breezes and told
them about his change of name
and asked them to tell all his
friends that in the future he
would not answer to the name of
Peter Rabbit, but only to the
name of Peter Cottontail. He was
very grave and earnest and important as he explained it to the
Merry Little Breezes. The Merry
Little Breezes kept their faces
straight while he was talking, but
as soon as they had left him to

carry his message they burst out laughing. It was such a joke!

And they giggled as they delivered this message to each of the little forest and meadow people:

> *"Peter Rabbit's changed his name.*
> *In the future without fail*
> *You must call him, if you please,*
> *Mr. Peter Cottontail."*

While they were doing this, Peter was back in the Old Briarpatch practicing new airs and trying to look very high and mighty and important, as became one with such a fine-sounding name as Peter Cottontail.

III

There's Nothing Like the Old Name After All

BOBBY COON and Jimmy Skunk had their heads together. Now when these two put their heads together, you may make up your mind that they are planning mischief. Yes, Sir, there is sure to be mischief afoot when Bobby Coon and Jimmy Skunk put their heads together as they were doing now. Had Peter Rabbit seen them, he might not have felt so easy in his mind as he did. But Peter didn't see them. He was too much taken up with trying to look as important as his new name sounded. He was putting on airs and holding his head very high as he went down to the Smiling Pool to call on Jerry Muskrat.

Whenever anyone called him by his old name, Peter pretended not to hear. He pretended that he had never heard that name and didn't know that he was being spoken to. Bobby Coon and Jimmy Skunk thought it a great joke and they made up their minds that they would have some

[25]

fun with Peter and perhaps make him see how very foolish he was. Yes, Sir, they planned to teach Peter a lesson. Bobby Coon hurried away to find Reddy Fox and tell him that Peter had gone down to the Smiling Pool, and that if he hid beside the path, he might catch Peter on the way back.

Jimmy Skunk hunted up Blacky the Crow and Sammy Jay and told them of his plan and what he wanted them to do to help. Of course they promised that they would. Then he went to Ol' Mistah Buzzard and told him. Ol' Mistah Buzzard grinned and promised that he would do his share. Then Bobby Coon and Jimmy Skunk hid where they could see all that would happen.

Peter had reached the Smiling Pool and now sat on the bank admiring his own reflection in the water and talking to Jerry Muskrat. He had just told Jerry that when his old name was called out he didn't hear it any more, when along came Blacky the Crow.

"Hello, Peter Rabbit! You're just the fellow I am looking for; I've a very important message for you," shouted Blacky.

Peter kept right on talking

[27]

with Jerry Muskrat just as if he
didn't hear, although he was
burning with curiosity to know
what the message was.

"I say, Peter Rabbit, are you
deaf?" shouted Blacky the Crow.

Jerry Muskrat looked up at
Blacky and winked. "Peter Rab-
bit isn't here," said he. "This is
Peter Cottontail."

"Oh!" said Blacky. "My message is for Peter Rabbit, and it's
something he really ought to
know. I'm sorry he isn't here."
And with that, away flew Blacky
the Crow, chuckling to himself.

Peter looked quite as uncomfortable as he felt, but of course

"I say, Peter Rabbit, are you deaf?"
shouted Blacky the Crow

he couldn't say a word after boasting that he didn't hear people who called him Peter Rabbit. Pretty soon along came Sammy Jay. Sammy seemed very much excited.

"Oh, Peter Rabbit, I'm so glad I've found you!" he cried. "I've some very important news for you."

Peter had all he could do to sit still and pretend not to hear, but he did.

"This is Peter Cottontail," said Jerry Muskrat, winking at Sammy Jay.

"Oh," replied Sammy, "my news is for Peter Rabbit!" And

off he flew, chuckling to himself.

Peter looked and felt more uncomfortable than ever. He bade Jerry Muskrat good-by and started for the dear Old Briar-patch to think things over. When he was halfway there, Ol' Mistah Buzzard came sailing down out of the sky.

"Brer Cottontail," said he, "if yo' see anything of Brer Rabbit, yo' tell him that Brer Fox am hiding behind that big bunch of grass just ahead."

Peter stopped short, and his heart gave a great leap. There, behind the clump of grass, was something red, sure enough.

[31]

Peter didn't wait to see more. He started for a hiding place he knew of in the Green Forest as fast as he could go, and behind him raced Reddy Fox. As he ran, he heard Blacky the Crow and Sammy Jay laughing, and then he knew that this was the news that they had had for him.

"I — I — guess that Peter Rabbit is a good enough name, after all," he panted.

IV

Peter Rabbit Fools Jimmy Skunk

PETER RABBIT came hopping and skipping down the Crooked Little Path. Unc' Billy Possum always calls him Brer Rabbit, but everybody else calls him Peter. Peter was feeling very fine that morning, very fine indeed. Every few minutes he jumped up in the air and kicked his heels together, just for fun. Presently he met Jimmy Skunk.

Jimmy was on his way back from Farmer Brown's cornfield, where he had been helping Blacky the Crow get free from a snare. Jimmy was still laughing over the way Blacky the Crow had been caught. He had to tell Peter Rabbit all about it.

Peter thought it just as good a joke as did Jimmy, and the two trotted along side by side, planning how they would spread the news, all over the Green Meadows, that Blacky the Crow, who thinks himself so smart, had been caught.

"That reminds me," said Jimmy Skunk suddenly, "I

[34]

haven't had my breakfast yet. Have you seen any beetles this morning, Peter Rabbit?"

Peter Rabbit stopped and scratched his long left ear with his long left hind foot.

"Now you speak of it, it seems to me that I did," said Peter Rabbit.

"Where?" asked Jimmy Skunk eagerly.

Peter pretended to think very hard.

"It seems to me that it was back at the top of the Crooked Little Path up the hill," said Peter.

"I think I will go look for them at once," replied Jimmy.

"All right," replied Peter, "I'll show you the way."

So up the Crooked Little Path hopped Peter Rabbit, and right behind him trotted Jimmy Skunk. By and by they came to an old pine stump. Peter Rabbit stopped. He put one hand on his lips.

"Hush!" whispered Peter. "I think there is a whole family of beetles on the other side of this stump. You creep around the other side, and I'll creep around this side. When I thump the ground, you spring right around and grab them before they can run away."

So Jimmy Skunk crept around one side of the stump, and Peter Rabbit crept around the other side. Suddenly Peter thumped the ground hard, twice. Jimmy Skunk was waiting and all ready to spring. When he heard those thumps, he sprang just as quickly as he could. What do you think happened?

Why, Jimmy Skunk landed thump! right on Reddy Fox, who was taking a sun nap on the other side of the pine stump!

"Ha, ha, ha," shouted Peter Rabbit, and started down the Crooked Little Path as fast as his long legs could take him.

V

Reddy Fox Gets into Trouble

REDDY FOX, curled up behind the big pine stump, was dreaming of a coop full of chickens, where there was no Bowser the Hound to watch over them. Suddenly something landed on him with a thump that knocked all his breath out. For an instant it frightened Reddy so that he just shook and shook. Then he got his senses together and dis-

[38]

covered that it was Jimmy Skunk who had jumped on him.

Jimmy was very polite. He begged Reddy's pardon. He protested that it was all a mistake. He explained how Peter Rabbit had played a trick on both of them, and how he himself was just looking for beetles for breakfast.

Now Reddy Fox is very quick-tempered and, as soon as he realized that he had been made the victim of a joke, he lost his temper completely. He glared at Jimmy Skunk. He was so angry that he stuttered.

"Y-y-you, y-y-y-you did that on p-purpose," said Reddy Fox.

[39]

"No such thing!" declared Jimmy Skunk. "I tell you it was a joke on the part of Peter Rabbit, and if you don't believe me, just look down there on the Green Meadows."

Reddy Fox looked. There sat Peter, his hands on his hips, his long ears pointed straight up to the blue sky, and his mouth wide open, as he laughed at the results of his joke.

Reddy shook his fist.

"Ha, ha, ha," shouted Peter Rabbit.

Reddy Fox looked hard at Jimmy Skunk, but like all the other little meadow and forest

people, he has a very great re-
spect for Jimmy Skunk, and
though he would have liked to
quarrel with Jimmy, he thought
it wisest not to. Instead, he
started after Peter Rabbit as fast
as his legs could go.

Now Reddy Fox can run very
fast, and when Peter saw him
coming, Peter knew that he would
have to use his own long legs to
the very best of his ability. Away
they went across the Green Meadows. Jimmy Skunk, sitting on top
of the hill, could see the white
patch on the seat of Peter Rabbit's trousers bobbing this way
and that way, and right behind

[*41*]

him was Reddy Fox. Now Peter Rabbit could run fast enough to keep away from Reddy for a while. You remember that Peter's eyes are so placed that he can see behind him without turning his head. So he knew when Reddy was getting too near.

In and out among the bushes along the edge of the Green Meadows they dodged, and the more he had to run, the angrier Reddy Fox grew. He paid no attention to where they were going; his whole thought was of catching Peter Rabbit.

Now, when Peter began to grow tired, he began to work over to-

*Peter knew when Reddy Fox was getting
too near*

ward Farmer Brown's cornfield, where he knew that Farmer Brown's boy was hiding with Bowser the Hound. Dodging this way and that way, Peter worked over to the fence corner where Jimmy Skunk had watched Blacky the Crow get caught in a snare. He let Reddy almost catch him, then he dodged out into the open cornfield, and Reddy, of course, followed him.

"Bow-wow, bow-wow-wow!"

Reddy did not need to turn to know what had happened. Bowser the Hound had seen him and was after him. Peter just ducked behind a big bunch of grass and sat down to get his breath, while Reddy started off as hard as he could go, with Bowser the Hound behind him.

VI

Reddy Fools Bowser the Hound

AWAY across the Green Meadows and up the hill through the Green Forest raced Reddy Fox at the top of his speed. Behind him, nose to the ground, came Bowser the Hound, baying at the top of his lungs. Reddy ran along an old stone wall and jumped as far out into the field as he could.

"I guess that will fool him for a while," panted Reddy, as he sat down to get his breath.

When Bowser came to the place where Reddy had jumped on the stone wall, he just grinned.

"That's too old a trick to fool me one minute," said Bowser to himself, and he just made a big circle, so that in a few minutes he had found Reddy's tracks again.

Every trick that Reddy had heard old Granny Fox tell about he tried, in order to fool Bowser the Hound, but it was of no use at all. Bowser seemed to know exactly what Reddy was doing, and wasted no time.

Reddy was beginning to get

[47]

worried. He was getting dreadfully out of breath. His legs ached. His big plumy tail, of which he is very, very proud, had become dreadfully heavy. Granny Fox had warned him never, never to run into the snug house they had dug unless he was obliged to save his life, for that would tell Bowser the Hound where they lived, and then they would have to move.

How Reddy did wish that wise old Granny Fox would come to his relief! He was running along the back of Farmer Brown's pasture, and he could hear Bowser the Hound altogether too near for comfort. He looked this way and he looked that way for a chance to escape. Just ahead of him he saw a lot of woolly friends. They were Farmer Brown's sheep. Reddy had a bright idea. Like a flash he sprang on the back of one of the sheep. It frightened the sheep as badly as Reddy had been frightened when Jimmy Skunk had landed on him that morning.

"Baa, baa, baa!" cried the sheep and started to run. Reddy hung on tightly, and away they raced across the pasture.

Now Bowser the Hound trusts wholly to his nose to follow

[*49*]

Reddy Fox or Peter Rabbit or his master, Farmer Brown's boy. So he did not see Reddy jump on the back of the sheep, and, of course, when he reached the place where Reddy had found his strange horse, he was puzzled. Round and round, and round and round Bowser worked in a circle, but no trace of Reddy could he find.

And all the time Reddy sat behind the stone wall on the far side of the pasture, getting his wind and laughing and laughing at the smart way in which he had fooled Bowser the Hound.

VII

Reddy Invites Peter Rabbit To Take a Walk

OLD Granny Fox was not feeling well. For three days she had been unable to go out hunting, and for three days Reddy Fox had tried to find something to tempt Granny's appetite. He had brought in a tender young chicken from Farmer Brown's henyard, and he had stolen a plump trout from Billy

Mink's storehouse, but Granny had just turned up her nose.

"What I need," said Granny Fox, "is a tender young rabbit."

Now Reddy Fox is very fond of Granny Fox, and when she said that she needed a tender young rabbit, Reddy made up his mind that he would get it for her, though how he was going to do it he didn't know. Dozens of times he had tried to catch Peter Rabbit, and every time Peter's long legs had taken him to a place of safety. "I'll just have to fool Peter Rabbit," said Reddy Fox, as he sat on his doorstep and looked over the Green Meadows.

[52]

Reddy Fox is very sly. He is so sly that it is hard work to be sure when he is honest and when he is playing a trick. As he sat on his doorstep, looking across the Green Meadows, he saw the Merry Little Breezes coming his way. Reddy smiled to himself. When they got near enough, he shouted to them.

"Will you do something for me?" he asked.

"Of course we will," shouted the Merry Little Breezes, who are always delighted to do something for others.

"I wish you would find Peter Rabbit and tell him that I have found a new bed of tender young carrots in Farmer Brown's garden, and invite him to go there with me tomorrow morning at sunup," said Reddy Fox.

Away raced the Merry Little Breezes to find Peter Rabbit and give him the invitation of Reddy Fox. Pretty soon back they came to tell Reddy that Peter Rabbit would be delighted to meet Reddy on the edge of the Old Briar-patch at sunup the next morning, and go with him to get some tender young carrots.

Reddy smiled to himself, for now he was sure that he would get Peter Rabbit for Granny.

[54]

Early the next morning, just
before sunup, Reddy Fox started
down the Lone Little Path and
hurried across the Green Meadows to the Old Briar-patch.
Reddy was dressed in his very
best suit of clothes, and very smart
and handsome he looked. When
he reached the Old Briar-patch he
could see nothing of Peter Rabbit.
He waited and waited and waited,
but still Peter Rabbit did not
come. Finally he gave it up and
decided that he would go over
and have a look at the young carrots in Farmer Brown's garden.
When he got there, what do you
think he saw? Why, all around

[55]

that bed of tender young carrots
were footprints, and the footprints
were Peter Rabbit's!

Reddy Fox ground his teeth
and snarled wickedly, for he knew
then that instead of fooling Peter
Rabbit, Peter Rabbit had fooled
him. Just then up came one of
the Merry Little Breezes of Old
Mother West Wind.

"Good morning, Reddy Fox,"
said the Merry Little Breeze.

"Good morning," replied Reddy
Fox, and if you could have seen
him and heard him, you would
never have suspected how ill-
tempered he was feeling.

"Peter Rabbit asked me to

come and tell you that he is very sorry that he could not meet you at the Briar-patch this morning, but that he grew so hungry thinking of those tender young carrots that he just had to come and get some before sunup, and he is very much obliged to you for telling him about them. He says they are the finest young carrots that he has ever tasted," said the Merry Little Breeze.

The heart of Reddy Fox was filled with rage, but he did not let the Merry Little Breeze know it. He just smiled and sent the Merry Little Breeze back to Peter Rabbit to tell him how glad he

[57]

was that Peter enjoyed the carrots, and to invite Peter to meet him the next morning on the edge of the Old Briar-patch at sunup, to go with him to a patch of sweet clover which he had just found near the old hickory tree.

The Merry Little Breeze danced off with the message. Pretty soon he was back to say that Peter Rabbit would be delighted to go to the sweet clover patch the next morning.

Reddy grinned as he trudged off home. "I'll just be at the clover patch an hour before sun-up tomorrow, and then we'll see!" he said to himself.

[58]

VIII

Peter Rabbit Gets an Early Breakfast

PETER RABBIT crept out of his snug little bed in the middle of the Old Briar-patch two hours before sunup and hurried over to the big hickory tree. Sure enough, close by, he found a beautiful bed of sweet clover, just as Reddy Fox had said was there. Peter chuckled to himself as he ate and ate and ate, until his little round stomach was so full that he could hardly hop.

When he had eaten all that he could, he hurried back to the Old Briar-patch to finish his morning nap, and all the time he kept chuckling to himself. You see, Peter was supicious of Reddy Fox, and so he had gone over to the sweet clover bed alone, two hours before sunup.

Peter Rabbit had hardly left the sweet clover bed when Reddy Fox arrived. Reddy lay down in the long meadow grass and grinned to himself as he waited. Slowly the minutes went by, until up from behind the Purple Hills

came jolly, round, red Mr. Sun —
but no Peter Rabbit. Reddy
stopped grinning.

"Perhaps," said he to himself,
"Peter is waiting for me on the
edge of the Old Briar-patch, and
wasn't going to try to fool me."

So Reddy hurried over to the
Old Briar-patch, and sure enough
there was Peter Rabbit sitting on
the edge of it. When Peter saw
him coming, he dodged in behind
a big clump of friendly old brambles. Reddy came up with his
broadest smile.

"Good morning, Peter Rabbit,"
said Reddy. "Shall we go over to
that sweet clover bed?"

[*61*]

Peter put one hand over his mouth to hide a smile. "Oh," said he, "I was so dreadfully hungry for sweet clover that I couldn't wait until sunup, and so I went over two hours ago. I hope you will excuse me, Reddy Fox. I certainly do appreciate your kindness in telling me of that new sweet clover bed, and I hope I have not put you out."

"Certainly not," replied Reddy Fox in his pleasantest manner, and you know Reddy Fox can be very pleasant indeed when he wants to be. "It is a very great pleasure to be able to give you pleasure. There is nothing I so like to do as to give pleasure to others. By the way, I have just heard that Farmer Brown has a new planting of young cabbage in the corner of his garden. Will you meet me here at sunup to-morrow morning to go over there?"

"I shall be delighted to, I shall indeed!" replied Peter Rabbit, and all the time he smiled to himself behind his hand.

Reddy Fox bade Peter Rabbit good-by in the pleasantest way you can imagine, yet all the time, down in his heart, Reddy was so angry that he hardly knew what to do, for you see, he had to go back to

[63]

Granny Fox without the tender young rabbit which he had promised her.

"This time I will be there two hours before sunup, and then we will see, Peter Rabbit, who is the smartest!" said Reddy Fox to himself.

IX

Reddy Fox Gets
a Scare

PETER RABBIT looked up at
the silvery moon and laughed
aloud. Then he kicked up his
heels and laughed again as he
started out across the Green
Meadows toward Farmer Brown's
garden. You see, Peter was suspicious, very supicious indeed, of
Reddy Fox. So, as it was a beautiful night for a walk, he thought
he would just run over to Farmer

Brown's garden and see if he could find that bed of newly planted cabbage, about which Reddy Fox had told him.

So Peter hopped and skipped across the Green Meadows, singing as he went:

"Hold, ol' Miss Moon, hold up your light!
Show the way! show the way!
The little stars are shining bright;
Night folks all are out to play."

When Peter reached Farmer Brown's garden, he had no trouble in finding the new planting of cabbage. It was tender. It was good. My, how good it was! Peter started in to fill his little round stomach. He ate and ate and ate and ate! By and by, just when he thought he couldn't eat another mouthful, he happened to look over to a patch of moonlight. For just a second Peter's heart stopped beating. There was Reddy Fox coming straight over to the new cabbage bed!

Peter Rabbit didn't know what to do. Reddy Fox hadn't seen him yet, but he would in a minute or two, unless Peter could hide. He was too far from the dear Old Briar-patch to run there Peter looked this way and looked that way. Ha! ha! There lay Farmer Brown's boy's old straw hat, just where he had left it when the supper horn blew. Peter crawled under it. It covered him completely.

Peter peeped out from under one edge. He saw Reddy Fox standing in the moonlight, looking at the bed of newly set cabbage. Reddy was smiling as if his thoughts were very pleasant. Peter shivered. He could just guess what Reddy was thinking — how he would gobble up Peter, when once he got him away from the safety of the Old Briar-patch.

The thought made Peter so indignant that he forgot that he was hiding, and he sat up on his hind legs. Of course he lifted the straw hat with him. Then he remembered and sat down again in a hurry. Of course the straw hat went down quite as quickly.

Presently Peter peeped out. Reddy Fox was staring and staring at the old straw hat, and he wasn't smiling now. He actually looked frightened. It gave Peter an idea. He made three long hops straight toward Reddy Fox, all the time keeping the old straw hat over him. Of course the hat went along with him, and, because it covered Peter all up, it looked for all the world as if the hat were alive.

Reddy Fox gave one more long

look at the strange thing coming toward him through the cabbage bed, and then he started for home as fast as he could go, his tail between his legs.

Peter Rabbit just lay down right where he was and laughed and laughed and laughed. And it almost seemed as if the old straw hat laughed too.

X

Peter Has Another Great Laugh

I⊤ WAS just sunup as Reddy
Fox started down the Lone
Little Path to the Green Mead-
ows. Reddy was late. He should
be over at the Old Briar-patch by
this time. He was afraid now that
Peter Rabbit would not be there.
When he came in sight of the
Old Briar-patch, there sat Peter
on the edge of it.

"Good morning, Peter Rabbit," said Reddy Fox in his politest manner. "I am sorry to have kept you waiting; it is all because I had a terrible fright last night."

"Is that so? What was it?" asked Peter, ducking down behind a big bramble bush to hide his smile.

"Why, I went over to Farmer Brown's garden to see if that new planting of young cabbage was all right, and there I met a terrible monster. It frightened me so that I did not dare to come out this morning until jolly, round, red Mr. Sun had begun to climb up in the sky, and so I am a little

*"Good morning, Peter Rabbit," said Reddy
in his politest manner*

late. Are you ready, Peter Rabbit, to go up to the new planting of young cabbage with me?" asked Reddy in his pleasantest manner.

Now, what do you think Peter Rabbit did? Why, Peter just began to laugh. He laughed and laughed and shouted! He lay down on his back and kicked his heels for very joy! But all the time he took care to keep behind a big, friendly bramble bush.

Reddy Fox stared at Peter Rabbit. He just didn't know what to make of it. He began to think that Peter had gone crazy. He couldn't see a thing to laugh at, yet here was Peter laughing fit to kill himself. Finally Peter stopped and sat up.

"Did — did — the monster catch you, Reddy Fox?" he asked, wiping his eyes.

"No," replied Reddy, "it didn't catch me, because I could run faster than it could, but it chased me all the way home."

"In that case, I think I'll not go up to the cabbage bed this morning, for you know I cannot run as fast as you can, Reddy, and the monster might catch me," replied Peter very gravely. "Besides," he added, "I have had my fill of tender young cabbage, and it was very nice indeed."

"What!" shouted Reddy Fox.

"Yes," continued Peter Rabbit, "I just couldn't wait till morning, so I went up there early last night. I'm much obliged to you for telling me of it, Reddy Fox; I am indeed."

For just a little minute an ugly look crept into Reddy's face, for now he knew that once more Peter Rabbit had fooled him. But he kept his temper and managed to smile, as he said:

"Oh, don't mention it, Peter Rabbit, don't mention it. But tell me, didn't you meet the monster?"

"No," replied Peter Rabbit.

And then, do what he would, he couldn't keep sober another minute, but began to laugh just as he had before.

"What's the joke, Peter Rabbit? Tell me so that I can laugh too," begged Reddy Fox.

"Why," said Peter Rabbit, when he could get his breath, "the joke is that the monster that frightened you so was the old straw hat of Farmer Brown's boy, and I was underneath it. Ha, ha, ha! Ho, ho, ho!"

Then Reddy Fox knew just how badly Peter Rabbit had fooled him. With a snarl he sprang right over the bramble

[77]

bush at Peter Rabbit, but Peter was watching, and darted away along one of his own special little paths through the Old Briar-patch. Reddy tried to follow, but the brambles tore his clothes and scratched his face and stuck in his feet. Finally he had to give it up. Torn and bleeding and angry, he turned back home, and as he left the Old Briar-patch, he could still hear Peter Rabbit laughing.

XI

Shadow the Weasel Gets Lost

ALL the Green Meadows had heard how Peter Rabbit had frightened Reddy Fox with an old straw hat, and everywhere that Reddy went someone was sure to shout after him:

> "Reddy Fox is fine to see;
>   He's as brave as brave can be
>   'Til he meets an old straw hat,
>   Then he don't know where he's at!"

[79]

Then Reddy would lose his temper and chase his tormentors. Most of all, he wanted to catch Peter Rabbit. He lay in wait for Peter in fence corners and behind bushes and trees, but somehow Peter seemed always to know that Reddy was there.

In the Old Briar-patch Peter was safe. Reddy had tried to follow him there, but he had found that it was of no use at all. Peter's paths were so narrow, and the brambles tore Reddy's clothes and scratched him so, that he had to give it up.

Reddy was thinking of this one day as he sat on his doorstep,

[80]

scowling over at the Old Briar-patch, and then all of a sudden he thought of Shadow the Weasel. Shadow is so slim that he can go almost anywhere that any-one else can, and he is so fierce that nearly all of the little meadow people are terribly afraid of him. Reddy smiled. It was a mean, wicked, crafty smile. Then he hopped up and hurried to find Shadow the Weasel and tell him his plan.

Shadow listened, and then he too began to smile. "It's easy, Reddy Fox, the easiest thing in the world! We'll get Peter Rabbit just as sure as fat hens are good eating," said he, as they started for the Old Briar-patch.

Reddy's plan was very simple. Shadow the Weasel was to follow Peter Rabbit along Peter's narrow little paths and drive Peter out of the Old Briar-patch onto the Green Meadows, where Reddy Fox could surely catch him.

So Reddy Fox sat down to wait while Shadow started into the Old Briar-patch. Peter Rabbit heard him coming and, of course, Peter began to run. Now, when Peter first made his home in the Old Briar-patch, he had foreseen that someday Shadow the Weasel might come to hunt him there, so Peter had made dozens and dozens of little paths, twisting and turning and crossing and re-crossing in the most puzzling way. Of course, Peter himself knew every twist and turn of every one of them, but Shadow had not gone very far before he was all mixed up. He kept his sharp little nose to the ground to smell Peter's footsteps, but Peter kept crossing his own tracks so often that pretty soon Shadow could not tell which path Peter had last taken.

Peter led him farther and farther into the middle of the Old Briar-patch. Right there Shadow

[83]

came to a great big puddle of water. Peter had jumped clear across it, for you know Peter's legs are long and meant for jumping.

Now Shadow hates to get his feet wet, and when he reached the puddle, he stopped. He glared with fierce little red eyes across at Peter Rabbit, sitting on the other side. Then he started around the edge.

Peter waited until Shadow was almost around, and then he jumped back across the puddle. There was nothing for Shadow to do but go back around, which he did. Of course, Peter just did the same thing over again, all the time laughing in his sleeve, for Shadow the Weasel was growing angrier and angrier. Finally he grew so angry that he tried to jump the puddle himself, and in he fell with a great splash!

When Shadow crawled out, wet and muddy, Peter had disappeared, and Shadow couldn't tell which path he had taken. Worse still, he didn't know which path to take to get out himself. He tried one after another, but after a little while he would find himself back at the puddle in the middle of the Old Briar-patch. Shadow the Weasel was lost! Yes, Sir,

*Shadow the Weasel tried to jump the puddle,
and in he fell with a splash*

Shadow the Weasel was lost in the Old Briar-patch.

Outside, Reddy Fox waited and watched, but no frightened Peter Rabbit came jumping out as he expected. What could it mean? After a long, long time he saw someone very muddy and very wet and very tired crawl out of one of Peter Rabbit's little paths. It was Shadow the Weasel.

Reddy took one good look at him and then he hurried away. He didn't want to hear what Shadow the Weasel would say. And as he hurried across the Green Meadows, he heard Peter

Rabbit's voice from the middle of the Old Briar-patch.

"If at first you don't succeed, try, try again!" shouted Peter Rabbit.

Reddy Fox ground his teeth.

XII

The Plot of Two Scamps

SAMMY JAY, looking around for mischief, found Reddy Fox sitting on his doorstep with his chin in both hands and looking as if he hadn't a friend in the world.

"What are you doing?" asked Sammy Jay.

"I'm just a-studying," replied Reddy Fox.

"What are you studying? Perhaps

I can help you," said Sammy Jay.

Reddy Fox heaved a long sigh. "I'm a-studying how I can catch Peter Rabbit," replied Reddy.

Sammy Jay scratched his head thoughtfully. Reddy Fox still sat with his chin in his hands and thought and thought and thought and thought. Sammy Jay sat on one foot and scratched and scratched and scratched his head with the other. Suddenly Sammy looked up.

"I have it!" said he. "You remember the hollow log over beyond the old hickory tree?"

Reddy nodded his head.

"Well, I'll go down and invite

[*90*]

Peter Rabbit to come over there and see the strangest thing in the world. You know what great curiosity Peter Rabbit has. Now, you be hiding in the hollow log, and when you hear me say to Peter Rabbit, 'The strangest thing in the world is waiting for you over there, Peter,' you spring out, and you'll have Peter."

Reddy Fox brightened up. This plan certainly did look good to Reddy. Peter had fooled him so many times that he was almost in despair. He knew that if he sent another invitation to Peter, Peter would suspect right away that it meant mischief. But Peter wouldn't think that Sammy Jay was planning mischief, because he knew that Sammy is the greatest news teller in the Green Forest.

So Reddy Fox trotted off to the hollow log down by the big hickory tree and crept inside. Sammy Jay flew over to the Old Briar-patch to look for Peter Rabbit. He found him sitting under a big bramble bush.

"Good morning, Peter Rabbit," said Sammy Jay, with his finest manner.

Peter looked at Sammy sharply as he returned his greeting. Sammy Jay wasn't in the habit of being so polite to Peter, and

Peter began to study just what it could mean.

"I saw the strangest thing in the world this morning," said Sammy Jay.

Peter pricked up his ears. In spite of himself, he began to grow curious. "What was it, Sammy Jay?" he asked.

Sammy looked very mysterious. "I really don't know what it is," he replied, "but I can show it to you, if you want to see for yourself, Peter Rabbit."

Of course Peter wanted to see it, so he started out across the Green Meadows with Sammy Jay. Now the farther he went, the

[93]

ADVENTURES OF PETER COTTONTAIL

more time he had to think, and by the time he had nearly reached the old hickory tree, Peter began to suspect a trick.

Sammy Jay motioned Peter to approach very carefully. "It's right over there, in that hollow log, Peter," he whispered. "You go peep in, and you'll see it." Then Sammy prepared to give the signal to Reddy Fox.

Peter hopped a couple of steps nearer, and then he sat up very straight and gazed at the hollow log. Somehow he didn't like the looks of it. He didn't know why, but he just didn't. Then along came one of Old Mother West

Wind's Merry Little Breezes, dancing right past the hollow log and up to Peter Rabbit, and with her she brought a funny smell.

Peter's little wobbly nose wrinkled. That funny smell certainly reminded Peter of Reddy Fox. He wrinkled his nose again. Then he suddenly whirled about. "Excuse me, Sammy Jay," he exclaimed. "I just remembered something very important!" And before Sammy Jay could open his mouth, Peter had started like a little brown streak for the Old Briar-patch.

XIII

Reddy Fox Comes to Life

REDDY FOX lay on the side hill. Bobby Coon found him there, and when Bobby spoke to him, Reddy made no reply. Bobby went over and looked at him. Reddy's eyes were closed. Bobby grinned to himself, then he tiptoed a little nearer and shouted "Boo" right in one of Reddy's little black ears. Still Reddy did not move. Bobby

Coon's face grew sober. He poked Reddy with his foot, but still Reddy did not move. Then he pulled Reddy's tail, and still Reddy did not move. "It must be that Reddy Fox is dead," thought Bobby Coon, and he hurried away to tell the news.

There was great excitement on the Green Meadows and in the Green Forest when the little people there heard that Reddy Fox was dead. Of course, everyone wanted to see Reddy, and soon there was a procession of little meadow and forest people hurrying across the Green Meadows to the hillside where Reddy

Soon there was a procession of little people
hurrying to where Reddy lay

Fox lay. Jimmy Skunk, Johnny Chuck, Billy Mink, Little Joe Otter, Unc' Billy Possum, Danny Meadow Mouse, Spotty the Turtle, Old Mr. Toad, Grandfather Frog, Jerry Muskrat, Sammy Jay, Blacky the Crow, Happy Jack Squirrel, Striped Chipmunk, Jumper the Hare, Prickly Porky, all were there. They formed a big circle around Reddy Fox.

Then they began to talk about Reddy. Some told of the good things that Reddy had done and what a fine gentleman he was. Others told of the mean things that Reddy Fox had done and how glad they were that they

[99]

would no longer have to watch out for him. It was surprising the number of bad things that were said. But then, they felt safe in saying them, for was not Reddy lying right there before them, stone dead?

Now Peter Rabbit had not heard the news until late in the day, and when he did hear it, he started as fast as his long legs could take him to have a last look at Reddy. Halfway there he suddenly stopped and scratched one of his long ears. Peter was thinking. It was mighty funny that Reddy Fox should have died without anyone having heard that

[*100*]

he was sick. Peter started on again, but this time he did not hurry. Presently he cut a long twig, which he carried along with him. When he reached the circle around Reddy Fox, he stole up behind Prickly Porky the Porcupine and whispered in his ear.

Prickly Porky took the long twig which Peter handed to him, while Peter went off at a little distance and climbed up on an old stump where he could see. Prickly Porky reached over and tickled one of Reddy's black ears. For a minute nothing happened. Then the black ear twitched. Prickly Porky tickled the end of

[101]

Reddy's little black nose; then he tickled it again. What do you think happened? Why, Reddy Fox sneezed!

My, my, my! How that circle around Reddy Fox did disappear! All the little people who were afraid of Reddy Fox scampered away as fast as they could run, while all the other little people who were not afraid of Reddy Fox began to laugh, and the one who laughed loudest of all was Peter Rabbit, as he started back to the Old Briar-patch.

Of course, Reddy Fox knew then that it was of no use at all to pretend that he was dead, so he sprang to his feet and started after Peter Rabbit at the top of his speed, but when he reached the Old Briar-patch, Peter was safely inside, and Reddy could hear him laughing as if he would split his sides.

"If at first you don't succeed, try, try again!" shouted Peter Rabbit.

XIV

Peter Rabbit in a Tight Place

"Hop along, skip along,
  The sun is shining bright;
Hum a song, sing a song,
  My heart is always light."

IT IS true, Peter Rabbit always is lighthearted. For days and days Reddy Fox had been trying to catch Peter, and Peter had had to keep his wits very sharp indeed in order to keep out of Reddy's way. Still, it didn't seem to worry

[*104*]

Peter much. Just now he was hopping and skipping down the Lone Little Path without a care in the world.

Presently Peter found a nice shady spot close by a big rock. Underneath one edge of the rock was a place just big enough for Peter to crawl in — it was just the place for a nap. Peter was beginning to feel sleepy, so he crawled in there and soon was fast asleep.

By and by Peter began to dream. He dreamed that he had gone for a long walk, way, way off from the safe Old Briar-patch, and that out from behind a big

[*105*]

bush had sprung Reddy Fox. Just as Reddy's teeth were about to close on Peter, Peter woke up. It was such a relief to find that he was really snug and safe under the big rock that he almost shouted aloud. But he didn't, and a minute later he was, oh, so glad he hadn't, for he heard a voice that seemed as if it were right in his ear. It was the voice of Reddy Fox. Yes, Sir, it was the voice of Reddy Fox.

Peter hardly dared to breathe, and you may be sure that he did not make even the smallest sound, for Reddy Fox was sitting on the very rock under which Peter was resting. Reddy Fox was talking to Blacky the Crow. Peter listened with all his might, for what do you think Reddy Fox was saying? Why, he was telling Blacky the Crow of a new plan to catch Peter Rabbit and was asking Blacky to help him.

Peter had never been so frightened in his life, for here was Reddy Fox so close to him that Peter could have reached out and touched one of Reddy's legs, as he kicked his heels over the edge of the big rock. By and by Blacky the Crow spoke.

"I saw Peter Rabbit coming down this way early this morning," said Blacky, "and I don't think he has gone home. Why don't you go over and hide near the Old Briar-patch and catch Peter when he comes back? I will watch out, and if I see Peter, I will tell him that you have gone hunting your breakfast way over beyond the big hill. Then he will not be on the watch."

"The very thing," exclaimed Reddy Fox, "and if I catch him, I will surely do something for you, Blacky. I believe that I will go right away."

Then the two rascals planned, and chuckled as they thought how they would outwit Peter Rabbit.

"I'm getting hungry," said Reddy Fox, as he arose and stretched. "I wonder if there is a field mouse hiding under this old rock. I believe I'll look and see."

Peter's heart almost stood still as he heard Reddy Fox slide down off the big rock. He wriggled himself still farther under the rock and held his breath. Just then Blacky the Crow gave a sharp "Caw, caw, caw!" That meant that Blacky saw something, and almost at once Peter heard a sound that sometimes filled his heart with fear but which now filled it with great joy. It was the voice of Bowser the Hound.

*He could see Reddy Fox running, and behind
him was Bowser the Hound*

Reddy Fox heard it, too, and he didn't stop to look under the big rock.

A little later Peter very cautiously crawled out of his resting place and climbed up where he could look over the Green Meadows. Way over on the far side he could see Reddy Fox running at the top of his speed, and behind him was Bowser the Hound.

"My! but that was a tight place," said Peter Rabbit, as he stretched himself.

[111]

XV

Johnny Chuck
Helps Peter

JOHNNY CHUCK had watched
Reddy Fox try to fool and
catch Peter Rabbit, and sometimes Johnny had been very
much afraid that Reddy would
succeed. But Peter had been too
smart for Reddy every time, and
Johnny had laughed with the
other little people of the Green
Meadows whenever the Merry
Little Breezes had brought a new

story of how Peter had outwitted Reddy.

"Peter'll have to watch out sharper than ever now, for Granny Fox is almost well, and she is very angry because Reddy could not catch Peter Rabbit for her when she was ill. She says that she is going to show that stupid Reddy how to do it and do it quickly," said Jimmy Skunk, when he stopped to chat with Johnny Chuck one fine morning.

Johnny had just been laughing very hard over one of Peter Rabbit's tricks, but now his face grew very sober, very sober indeed. "It won't do to let old Granny Fox catch Peter. It won't do at all. We must all turn in and help Peter," said Johnny. "Why, what would the Green Meadows and the Green Forest be like with no Peter Rabbit?" he added.

Late that afternoon Johnny Chuck happened to find Peter Rabbit taking a nap. Yes, Sir, Peter had actually gone to sleep outside the dear Old Briar-patch. At first Johnny thought that he would waken him and tell him that Reddy Fox was hunting right near. But just then Johnny's bright eyes saw something that made him chuckle. It was the home of some hot-tempered friends of his, a beautiful home made of what looked like gray paper. It was fastened to a bush just above a little path leading to the very spot where Peter lay fast asleep. Johnny chuckled again, then off he hurried. He sat down on top of a little hill. Pretty soon Reddy Fox came along through the hollow below.

"Hello, Reddy Fox! Do you want to know how you can catch Peter Rabbit?" asked Johnny.

Reddy looked up. He didn't know just what to say. He knew that Johnny Chuck and Peter had always been the very best of friends. Still, friends fall out

[115]

sometimes, and perhaps Johnny and Peter had. Reddy decided that he would be polite.

"I certainly do, Johnny Chuck," he replied. "Can you tell me how to do it?"

"Yes," said Johnny. "Peter is fast asleep over yonder behind that little bunch of huckleberry bushes. There is a little path through them. All you have to do is to hurry up that little path as fast and as still as you can."

Reddy Fox waited to hear no more. His eyes glistened as he started off at the top of his speed up the little path. Just as Johnny had expected, Reddy went in such a hurry that he didn't use his eyes for anything but signs of Peter Rabbit.

Bang! Reddy had run head first into the paper house of Johnny Chuck's hot-tempered friends. In fact he had smashed the whole side in. Out poured old Mrs. Hornet and all her family, and they had their little needles with them. Reddy forgot all about Peter Rabbit. He yelled at the top of his lungs and started for home, slapping at old Mrs. Hornet, whom he never could hit, and stopping every few minutes to roll over and over.

Of course, when he yelled, Peter

*Bang! Reddy had run head first into the house
of Old Mrs. Hornet*

Rabbit awoke and sat up to see what all the fuss was about. He saw Reddy running as if his life depended upon it. Over on the little hill he saw Johnny Chuck laughing so that the tears ran down his face. Then Peter began to laugh, too, and ran over to ask Johnny Chuck to tell him all about it.

XVI

Reddy Fox Tells a Wrong Story

REDDY FOX was a sight! There was no doubt about that. When he started down onto the Green Meadows that morning he limped like an old, old man. Yes indeed, Reddy was a sorry-looking sight. His head was swelled so that one eye was closed, and he could hardly see out of the other. Reddy never would have ventured out but that he just had to have

some fresh mud from the Smiling
Pool.

Reddy had waited until most
of the little meadow people were
out of the way. Then he had tried
to hurry so as to get back again
as quickly as possible.

But Johnny Chuck's sharp eyes
had spied Reddy, and Johnny had
guessed right away what the
trouble was. He hurried over to
tell Peter Rabbit. Then the two
little scalawags hunted up Jimmy
Skunk and Bobby Coon to tell
them, and the four hid near the
Lone Little Path to wait for
Reddy's return.

Pretty soon Reddy came limping along. Even Johnny Chuck was surprised at the way Reddy's face had swelled. It was plastered all over with mud, and he was a sorry sight indeed.

Bobby Coon appeared very much astonished to see Reddy in such condition, though of course Johnny Chuck had told him all about how Reddy had run head first into the home of old Mrs. Hornet and her family the day before.

Bobby stepped out in the Lone Little Path.

"Why, Reddy Fox, what has happened to you?" he exclaimed.

Reddy didn't see the others

"Why, Reddy Fox, what has happened to you?"
exclaimed Bobby Coon

hiding in the long grass. He didn't want Bobby Coon to know that he had been so careless as to run his head into a hornets' nest, so he told a wrong story. He put on a long face. That is, it was as long as he could make it, considering that it was so swelled.

"I've had a most terrible accident, Bobby Coon," said Reddy, sighing pitifully. "It happened yesterday as I was returning from an errand over beyond the hill. Just as I was coming through the deepest part of the wood, I heard someone crying. Of course I stopped to find out what the matter was."

[124]

"Of course!" interrupted Bobby Coon. "Certainly! To be sure! Of course!"

Reddy looked at him suspiciously, but went on with his tale. "Right down in the thickest, blackest place I found one of Unc' Billy Possum's children being worried to death by Digger the Badger. I couldn't see that little Possum hurt."

"Of course not!" broke in Bobby Coon.

"So I jumped in and tackled Old Man Badger, and I had him almost whipped, when I slipped over the edge of a big rock on the side of the hill. It took the

[125]

skin off my face and bruised me something terrible. But I don't care, so long as I saved that little Possum child," concluded Reddy, as he started on.

Johnny Chuck stole up behind him and thrust a sharp briar into the seat of Reddy's pants. At the same time Johnny made a noise like a whole family of hornets. Reddy Fox forgot his limp. He never even turned his head to look behind. Instead, he started off at his best speed, and it wasn't until he heard a roar of laughter behind him that he realized that he had been fooled again.

XVII

Reddy Almost Gets Peter Rabbit

REDDY FOX really was almost ill from the effects of the stings which old Mrs. Hornet and her family had given him when he knocked in the side of their house. For several days he limped around, his head badly swollen. Yes, Sir, Reddy Fox was in a dreadful bad way. The worst of it was that none of the other little meadow and forest people seemed to be the least bit sorry for him. Some of them actually laughed at him. Peter Rabbit did. Reddy Fox had made life very uncomfortable for Peter for a long time, and now Peter was actually enjoying Reddy's discomfort.

Now, while he was laid up this way, Reddy had plenty of time to think. He noticed that when he went out to walk, all those who kept at a safe distance when he was well now hardly got out of his way. They knew that he felt too sore and mean to try to catch them. Peter Rabbit hardly turned out of his path. A bright idea came to Reddy. He would continue to appear to feel badly, even after he was well. He would keep his head bound up and would limp down to the Smiling Pool for some mud every day. Then, when Peter Rabbit came near enough, Reddy would catch him.

So day after day Reddy limped down to the Smiling Pool. He kept his head tied up as if it were as bad as ever, and as he walked, he groaned as if in great pain. Even some of those who hated him most began to feel a little bit sorry for Reddy Fox. Peter has a very soft heart, and although he knew that Reddy Fox would

[*129*]

like nothing better than to gobble him up, he began to feel sorry for Reddy.

One morning Peter sat just outside the Old Briar-patch, when Reddy came limping along. He looked more miserable than usual. Just as it had been for several days, one of Reddy's eyes was closed.

"It must be hard work to see with only one eye," said Peter.

"It is," replied Reddy with a great sigh. "It is very hard work indeed."

"I don't see how you manage to get enough to eat," continued Peter, in his most sympathetic voice.

Reddy sighed again. "I don't, Peter Rabbit. I don't get enough to eat, and I'm nearly starved this very minute."

When he said this, such a note of longing crept into his voice that Peter instantly grew suspicious. While he was sorry for Reddy, he had no desire to make Reddy feel better by furnishing himself for a meal. Peter hopped around to the blind side of Reddy and turned his back to him, as he inquired for the health of old Granny Fox.

Now, you know that Peter's eyes are so placed in his head that he can see behind him without turning his head. Reddy Fox did not know this, or if he did he had forgotten it. Very slowly and craftily the closed eye opened a wee bit, and in that line of yellow was a hungry look. Peter Rabbit saw it and with a great jump landed behind a friendly bramble bush in the Old Briar-patch.

"Ha! ha!" shouted Peter, "I'd rather talk with you, Reddy Fox, when you haven't got a closed eye with such a hungry look in it. Ta, ta!"

Reddy Fox just shook his fist at Peter Rabbit, and started off home, pulling the bandage from his head as he went.

[132]

XVIII

Johnny Chuck
Prepares for Winter

THERE was something in the air that Peter Rabbit could not understand. It made him feel frisky and happy and ready to run a race or have a frolic with anyone who might happen along. He couldn't understand why it didn't make all his friends and neighbors on the Green Meadows and in the Green Forest feel the same way. But it didn't. No, Sir, it didn't. Some of those with whom he best liked to play wouldn't play at all, not even for a few minutes; said they hadn't time. Peter was puzzling over it as he scampered down the Lone Little Path, kicking his heels and trying to jump over his own shadow. Just ahead of him, sitting on his own doorstep, sat Johnny Chuck.

"My goodness, how fat Johnny Chuck is getting!" thought Peter Rabbit. Then he shouted, "Come on and play hide-and-seek, Johnny Chuck!"

But Johnny Chuck shook his

"Come and play hide-and-seek, Johnny Chuck!"
shouted Peter

head. "Can't!" said he. "I've got to get ready for winter."

Peter Rabbit sat down and looked at Johnny Chuck curiously. He couldn't understand why anybody should take the trouble to get ready for winter. He didn't, except that he put on a warmer coat. So he couldn't imagine why Johnny Chuck should have to get ready for winter.

"How do you do it?" he asked.

"Do what?" Johnny Chuck looked up in surprise.

"Why, get ready for winter, of course," Peter replied, just a wee bit impatiently.

Johnny Chuck looked at Peter

[*136*]

as if he thought Peter very stupid indeed.

"Why, I eat, of course," said he shortly, and began to stuff himself as if he hadn't had anything to eat for a week, when all the time he was so fat and roly-poly that he could hardly waddle.

Peter's eyes twinkled. "I should think you did!" he exclaimed. "I wouldn't mind getting ready for winter that way myself." You know Peter thinks a very great deal of his stomach. Then he added, "I should think you were trying to eat enough to last you all winter."

Johnny Chuck yawned sleepily and then once more began to eat.

"I am," he said briefly, talking with his mouth full.

"What's that?" cried Peter Rabbit, his big eyes popping out.

"I said I'm trying to eat enough to last me all winter! That's the way I get ready for winter," replied Johnny Chuck, just a wee bit crossly. "I think I've got enough now," he added. "How cool it is getting! I think I'll go down and go to sleep. I'll see you in the spring, Peter Rabbit."

"Wha — what's that?" exclaimed Peter Rabbit, looking as if he thought he hadn't heard aright. But Johnny Chuck had disappeared inside his house.

XIX

Peter Rabbit Gets Another Surprise

PETER RABBIT sat on Johnny Chuck's doorstep for five long minutes, scratching his head first with one hand, then with the other.

"Now, what did Johnny Chuck mean by saying that he would see me in the spring?" said Peter Rabbit to himself. "Here it isn't winter yet, and it will be a long, long time before spring, yet Johnny

Chuck spoke just as if he didn't expect to see me until winter has passed. Is he going away somewhere? If he isn't, why won't I see him all winter, just as I have all summer?"

The more Peter thought about it, the more puzzled he became. At last he had a happy thought. "I'll just run down to the Smiling Pool and ask Grandfather Frog. He is very old and very wise, and he will surely know what Johnny Chuck meant."

So, kicking up his heels, Peter Rabbit started down the Lone Little Path, lipperty-lipperty-lip, across the Green Meadows to the

Smiling Pool. There he found Grandfather Frog sitting as usual on his big lily pad, but the lily pad wasn't as green as it used to be, and Grandfather Frog didn't look as smart as usual. His big, goggly eyes looked heavy and dull, just as if they didn't see much of anything at all. Grandfather Frog nodded sleepily and once nearly fell off the big lily pad.

"Good morning, Grandfather Frog!" shouted Peter Rabbit.

"Eh? What?" said Grandfather Frog, blinking his eyes and putting one hand behind an ear, as if he were hard of hearing.

"I said good morning, Grandfather Frog!" shouted Peter Rabbit, a little louder than before.

"No," replied Grandfather Frog grumpily, "it isn't a good morning; it's too chilly." He shivered as he spoke.

Peter Rabbit pretended not to notice how grumpy grandfather Frog was. In his most polite way he asked, "Can you tell me, Grandfather Frog, where Johnny Chuck spends the winter?"

"Spends it at home, of course. Don't bother me with such foolish questions!" snapped Grandfather Frog.

"But if he is going to spend

[*142*]

the winter at home, what did he mean by saying that he would see me in the spring, just as if he didn't expect to see me before then?" persisted Peter Rabbit.

Grandfather Frog yawned, shook himself, yawned again, and said:

"Johnny Chuck probably meant just what he said, and I think I'll follow his example. It's getting too cold for an old fellow like me. I begin to feel it in my bones. I'm getting so sleepy that I guess the sooner I hunt up my bed in the mud at the bottom of the Smiling Pool, the better. Chugarum!

[143]

Johnny Chuck is wise. I'll see
you in the spring, Peter Rabbit,
and tell you all about it."

And with that, Grandfather
Frog dived with a great splash
into the Smiling Pool.

XX

Peter Tries Ol' Mistah Buzzard

PETER RABBIT sat on the edge
of the Smiling Pool and stared
at the place where Grandfather
Frog had disappeared with a great
splash. He watched the tiny waves
spread out in rings that grew
bigger and bigger and then
finally disappeared too. Now what
did Grandfather Frog mean when
he said, "I'll see you in the
spring, Peter Rabbit"? Johnny

[145]

Chuck had said that very same thing as he had gone down the long hall of his snug house, yet it would be a long, long time before spring, for it was not winter yet. Where did they expect to be all winter, and what did they expect to do? The more Peter puzzled over it, the less he could understand it.

> "My head is whirling round and round,
> So many funny things I've found;
> Folks say it grows too cold to stay,
> Yet do not seem to go away.
> They talk of meeting in the spring
> But don't explain a single thing.

"They just go into their houses and say good-by. I don't understand it at all, at all," said Peter

Rabbit, staring at the big lily pad on which Grandfather Frog had sat all summer, watching for foolish green flies to come his way. Somehow that big lily pad made Peter Rabbit feel terribly lonely. Then he had a happy thought.

"I'll just run over and ask Ol' Mistah Buzzard what it all means; he'll be sure to know," said Peter Rabbit, and off he started, lipperty-lipperty-lip, for the Green Forest.

When Peter got where he could see the tall dead tree that Ol' Mistah Buzzard had made his favorite resting place, he could see Ol' Mistah Buzzard stretching his big wings, as if he were getting ready to fly. Peter hurried faster. He didn't want Mistah Buzzard to get away before he could ask him what Johnny Chuck and Grandfather Frog had meant. Peter couldn't shout, because he hasn't much of a voice, you know, and then he was out of breath, anyway. So he just made those long legs of his go as fast as ever they could, which is very fast indeed.

Just as Peter Rabbit almost reached the tall dead tree, Ol' Mistah Buzzard jumped off the branch he had been sitting on, gave two or three flaps with his great wings, and then, spreading them out wide, began to sail round and round and up and up, as only Ol' Mistah Buzzard can.

"Wait! Wait! Please wait!" panted Peter Rabbit, but his voice was so weak that Ol' Mistah Buzzard didn't hear him. He saw Peter, however, but of course he didn't know that Peter wanted to talk with him. With a long swoop, Ol' Mistah Buzzard sailed off right over Peter's head.

"Good-by, Brer Rabbit; Ah'll see yo' in the spring!" said Ol' Mistah Buzzard, and before Peter could say a word, he was out of hearing up in the sky.

[*149*]

Peter watched him go up and up until he was just a speck in the blue, blue sky.

"Now what did he mean by that? Is he going to stay up in the sky until spring?" asked Peter Rabbit of himself. But not knowing, of course he couldn't answer.

XXI

Happy Jack Squirrel Is Too Busy To Talk

PETER RABBIT sat with his mouth wide open staring up into the blue, blue sky, where Ol' Mistah Buzzard was growing smaller and smaller. Finally he was just a teeny, weeny speck, and then Peter couldn't see him at all. Peter hitched up his trousers and sat for a long time, looking very thoughtful. He was troubled in his mind, was Peter

[*151*]

Rabbit. First Johnny Chuck had said, "I'll see you in the spring," and had disappeared underground; then Grandfather Frog had said, "I'll see you in the spring," and had disappeared in the Smiling Pool; now Ol' Mistah Buzzard had said, "Ah'll see yo' in the spring," and had disappeared up in the blue, blue sky.

"And they all spoke just as if they meant it," said Peter to himself. "I believe I'll go over and see Happy Jack Squirrel. Perhaps he can tell me what it all means."

So off started Peter Rabbit, lipperty-lipperty-lip, through the Green Forest, looking for Happy Jack Squirrel. Pretty soon he caught a glimpse of Happy Jack's gray coat.

"Hi, Happy Jack!" called Peter, hurrying as fast as he could.

"Hello, Peter Rabbit! Don't bother me this morning. I've got too much to do to be bothered," said Happy Jack, digging a little hole in the ground while he talked.

Peter grew curious at once, so curious that he forgot all about what he was going to ask Happy Jack. He sat down and watched Happy Jack put a nut in the hole and cover it up. Then Happy Jack hurried to dig another hole and do the same thing over again.

"What are you doing that for?" asked Peter Rabbit.

"Doing it for? Why, I'm getting ready for winter, of course, stupid!" said Happy Jack, as he paused for breath.

"But I thought you stored your nuts and corn in a hollow tree!" exclaimed Peter Rabbit.

"So I do," replied Happy Jack, "but I would be foolish to put all my supplies in one place, so I bury some of them."

"But how do you remember where you bury them?" persisted Peter.

"I don't always, but when I forget, my nose helps me out. Then I just dig down and get

[154]

them," said Happy Jack. "Now I can't stop to talk any more, for I am late this year, and the first thing I know, winter will be here."

Then Peter remembered what he had come for. "Oh, Happy Jack, what did Johnny Chuck and Grandfather Frog and Ol' Mistah Buzzard mean by saying that they would see me in the spring?" he cried.

"Can't stop to tell you now!" replied Happy Jack, running this way and that way, and pulling over the fallen leaves to hunt for another nut. "Winter's coming, and I've got to be ready for it. Can't stop to talk."

And that was all Peter Rabbit could get out of him, although he followed Happy Jack about and bothered him with questions until Happy Jack quite lost his temper. Peter sighed. He saw Chatterer the Red Squirrel and Striped Chipmunk both quite as busy as Happy Jack.

"It's of no use to ask them, for they are doing the same thing that Happy Jack is," thought Peter. "I don't see the use of all this fuss about winter, anyway. I don't have to get ready for it. I believe I'll go down to the Smiling Pool again and see if maybe Grandfather Frog has come up."

[156]

XXII

Unc' Billy Possum
Explains Things

PETER RABBIT had sat still all
day long in his safe hiding
place in the middle of the dear
Old Briar-patch. Jolly, round, red
Mr. Sun had gone to bed behind
the Purple Hills, and the black
shadows had raced out across the
Green Meadows and into the
Green Forest. Now the moonlight
was driving them back a little
way. Peter hopped out of the
Old Briar-patch into the moon-

[*157*]

light and stretched first one leg and then another. Then he jumped up and down three or four times to get the kinks out of his long hind legs, and finally started off up the Lone Little Path, lipperty-lipperty-lip.

Halfway up the Lone Little Path Peter almost ran headlong into Unc' Billy Possum.

"Mah goodness, Brer Rabbit, yo'all done give me a powerful start!" exclaimed Unc' Billy. "What yo'all in such a right smart hurry fo'?"

Peter Rabbit grinned as he stopped running. "I didn't mean to frighten you, Uncle Billy. The fact is, I was on my way up to your house to see how you and old Mrs. Possum and all the children do this fine fall weather," said Peter Rabbit.

Unc' Billy Possum looked at Peter Rabbit sharply. "Seems to me that yo'all have taken a powerful sudden interest in we-alls. Ah don' remember seeing yo' up our way fo' a long time, Brer Rabbit," said he.

Peter looked a little foolish, for it was true that he hadn't been near Unc' Billy's hollow tree for a long time. "You see, I've been very busy getting ready for winter," said Peter, by way of an excuse.

Unc' Billy began to chuckle

*Unc' Billy Possum began to chuckle and
then to laugh*

and then to laugh. He rested both hands on his knees and laughed and laughed.

Peter Rabbit couldn't see anything to laugh at and he began to get just a wee bit provoked.

"What's the joke?" he demanded.

"The very idea of Brer Rabbit getting ready for winter or of being busy about anything but other people's affairs!" cried Unc' Billy, wiping his eyes.

Peter tried to feel and look very angry, but he could not. The very twinkle in Unc' Billy Possum's eyes made Peter want to laugh, too. In fact Peter just had

[*161*]

to laugh. Finally both stopped laughing, and Peter told Unc' Billy all about the things that had troubled him.

"Johnny Chuck disappeared down in his house and said he would see me in the spring; what did he mean by that?" asked Peter.

"Just what he said," replied Unc' Billy. "He done gone down to his bed and gone to sleep, and he's gwine to stay asleep until next spring."

Peter's eyes looked as if they would pop right out of his head. "And Grandfather Frog, what has become of him?" he asked.

[*162*]

"Oh, Grandfather Frog, he done gone to sleep, too, down in the mud at the bottom of the Smiling Pool. Ah reckon yo' will see Grandfather Frog come up right pert in the spring," said Unc' Billy.

"And Ol' Mistah Buzzard — he shouted down from the blue, blue sky that he would see me in the spring; has he gone to sleep up there?" asked Peter.

Unc' Billy Possum threw back his head and laughed fit to kill himself.

"Bless yo' long ears, no, Brer Rabbit! No indeed! Oh my, no! Brer Buzzard done fly away down

[*163*]

Souf to ol' Virginny to stay through the cold winter. And Ah 'most wish Ah was right along with him," added Unc' Billy, suddenly growing sober.

Then Peter Rabbit had a sudden thought. "You aren't going away to sleep all winter, are you, Uncle Billy?" he asked anxiously.

The grin came back to Unc' Billy's face. "No, Brer Rabbit. Ah reckons yo'all can find me right in mah hollow tree most any time this winter, if yo' knock loud enough. But Ah don' reckon on going out much, and Ah do reckon Ah'm going to have a right smart lot of sleep," replied Unc' Billy.

Peter Rabbit Has a Bright Idea

PETER RABBIT had a bright idea. At least Peter thought it was, and he chuckled over it a great deal. The more he thought about it, the better it seemed. What was it? Why, to follow the plan of Johnny Chuck and Grandfather Frog to avoid the cold, stormy weather by sleeping all winter. Yes, Sir, that was Peter Rabbit's bright idea.

[165]

"If Johnny Chuck can sleep and sleep
  The whole long, stormy winter through,
It ought to be, it seems to me,
  The very thing for me to do."

Peter Rabbit said this to himself, as he sat in the middle of the Old Briar-patch, chewing the end of a straw. If Johnny Chuck could do it, of course he could do it. All he would have to do would be to find a snug, warm house which nobody else was using, fix himself a comfortable bed, curl up, and go to sleep. Peter tried to picture himself sleeping away while the snow lay deep all over the Green Meadows and the Smiling Pool could smile

[*166*]

no more because the ice, the hard, black ice, would not let it.

Finally Peter could sit still no longer. He just had to tell someone about his bright idea and — and — well, he wasn't quite sure of just the way to go to sleep and sleep so long, for never in his life had Peter Rabbit slept more than a very, very short time without waking to see that no danger was near.

"I'll just run up and see Uncle Billy Possum!" said Peter.

Unc' Billy Possum was sitting in his doorway in his big hollow tree in the Green Forest when Peter Rabbit came hurrying up,

[*167*]

lipperty-lipperty-lip. Peter hardly waited to say good morning before he began to tell Unc' Billy all about his bright idea. Unc' Billy listened gravely, although there was a twinkle in his eyes.

"The first thing yo' must do is to find a warm place to sleep, Brer Rabbit," said Unc' Billy.

"Oh, that's easy enough!" said Peter.

"And then yo' must get fat, Brer Rabbit," continued Unc' Billy.

"What's that?" exclaimed Peter Rabbit, looking very much puzzled.

"Ah say yo' must get fat," re-

[168]

"And then you must get fat, Brer Rabbit,"
continued Unc' Billy

peated Unc' Billy, slapping his own fat sides.

"What for?" asked Peter.

"To keep yo' warm while yo' are asleep," replied Unc' Billy.

"Must I get very fat?" Peter asked.

"Yes, Sah, yo' must get very fat indeed," said Unc' Billy, and smiled, for it was hard to think of Peter Rabbit as very fat.

"How — how can I get fat?" asked Peter, and looked just a little bit worried.

"By eating and eating and eating, and between times sitting still," replied Unc' Billy Possum.

"That's easy, at least the eating

is!" said Peter, who you know thinks a great deal of his stomach. "Is that all, Uncle Billy?"

"That's about all, except yo' mustn't have anything on yo' mind when yo' try to go to sleep, Brer Rabbit. Yo' mustn't get to worrying fo' fear Brer Fox gwine to find yo' while yo' are asleep," said Unc' Billy, and grinned when Peter happened to turn his head.

Peter thanked Unc' Billy and hurried back to the Old Briar patch to think over all that Unc' Billy had told him.

"I certainly will try it," said Peter.

[*171*]

XXIV

Peter Prepares for a Long Sleep

DAY after day Peter Rabbit ran about this way and that over the Green Meadows and through the Green Forest, as if he had something on his mind. Jimmy Skunk noticed it. So did Billy Mink and Bobby Coon. But Peter would not stop to explain. Indeed, he was always in such a hurry that he wouldn't stop at all, but when he met them would shout "Hello!" over his shoulder and keep right on running, lipperty-lipperty-lip. Unc' Possum was the only one who guessed what it meant.

Unc' Billy grinned as he watched Peter running about with such a serious and important air. "Brer Rabbit is trying dreadful hard to fool hisself. Ah reckon he's looking fo' a place to curl up and try to sleep all winter," said Unc' Billy.

Unc' Billy had guessed just right. Peter was looking for a place to curl up to sleep all winter. Peter was too lazy to dig a new house for himself. Then it

[*173*]

was too late in the fall, anyway. He would just find some old, deserted house that some of Jimmy Skunk's relatives or Johnny Chuck's relations had given up using. So Peter went poking into every old house he knew of, trying to find one that wasn't so tumble-down that it wouldn't do. At last he found one that he thought would be just the place, and Peter chuckled to himself as he planned how he would curl up in the bedchamber, way down at the end of the long hall.

"Nobody'll ever guess where I am!" he said to himself and laughed aloud.

[*174*]

Then Peter remembered that Unc' Billy Possum had told him that it was necessary to eat a great deal so as to be very fat before going to sleep, for that was the way to keep warm all winter. So Peter started out to grow fat. This would be fun, the very best kind of fun, for there is nothing Peter Rabbit loves more than to fill his stomach, unless it is to satisfy his curiosity.

> Peter Rabbit's stomach is
> A thing that's most amazing;
> It takes so long to fill it up
> His time is short for lazing.

Perhaps this is the reason why, when Peter isn't eating, he wants

[175]

to loaf around and watch other people work. Anyway, Peter is a tremendous eater, and now that he wanted to grow fat, he felt that he must eat more than ever. So he began at once to eat and eat and eat. But there was one very important thing that Peter had forgotten. He had quite forgotten that it was now late in the fall, and the tender, young, green things which Peter dearly loves to eat were gone. He could no longer go down to the sweet clover patch and fill himself full to bursting. Farmer Brown had taken away all the cabbages and carrots and turnips that had made his garden so attractive to Peter.

So now Peter had to hunt for what he had to eat. That made a great deal of running about, and it is very hard work to grow fat when one runs about. The more Peter ate, the more he had to hunt for his food; and the more he had to hunt for his food, the more he had to run about; and the more he had to run about, the more he hurried and the faster he ran. Now, of course, running takes fat off.

"Oh dear!" cried Peter Rabbit. "Getting fat is not as easy as I thought!"

XXV

Unc' Billy Possum
Plays a Joke

---

*"Some folks never seem to be
Satisfied or quite content;
Always wanting something more
That fo' them was never meant."*

UNC' BILLY POSSUM said this to
himself as he watched Peter
Rabbit hurrying about through
the Green Forest and over the
Green Meadows, eating as fast as
ever he could so as to grow fat
that he might keep warm while

he slept all winter. Now Unc'
Billy Possum knew perfectly well
that Peter Rabbit couldn't sleep
all winter as Johnny Chuck does,
for Old Mother Nature had never
planned that Peter should. But
Unc' Billy knew that it was of no
use to tell Peter that, for Peter
wouldn't believe him. So he
chuckled as he watched Peter
rush around hunting for food
and actually running off what
little fat he did have, instead of
putting on more.

Of course, it just happened
that Unc' Billy Possum was right
over near the old house built by
Grandfather Skunk a long time

[*179*]

ago, which Peter Rabbit had decided to sleep in all winter. It just happened that he saw Peter when he finally went down to the little bedchamber at the end of the long hall to curl up and try to go to sleep.

Unc' Billy grinned. Then he chuckled. Finally he laughed until his fat sides shook.

"Ah reckon Ah'm gwine to have some fun with Brer Rabbit," said Unc' Billy, still chuckling, as he trotted off through the Green Forest. He went over to Bobby Coon's house and found Bobby, who had been out all night, just getting ready for bed.

[180]

But Bobby is always ready to play a joke, and when Unc' Billy told him about Peter Rabbit and what fun it would be to give Peter a scare, Bobby scrambled down from his hollow tree right away. Then they hunted up Jimmy Skunk, and the three started for the old house of Grandfather Skunk, where Peter Rabbit was trying to go to sleep for the winter.

"Ah done tell Peter that when he tried to go to sleep he mustn't get to thinking about what would happen if Brer Fox should jes' happen along and find him asleep. Ah reckons that that is

[*181*]

the very first thing Peter did think of, as soon as he curled himself up, and that he's thinking of it more'n ever right this blessed minute. Yo'alls wait while Ah listen at the door."

Unc' Billy stole very softly to the door of the old house. Then he began to grin and beckoned to Bobby Coon and Jimmy Skunk to come listen. They could hear long sighs from way down in the bedchamber at the end of the long hall. They heard Peter twist and turn, as he tried to make himself comfortable. But when they heard him saying a verse over and over to try to

[*182*]

*Unc' Billy stole very softly to the door
of the old house*

make himself go to sleep, they had to clap their hands over their mouths to keep from laughing out loud.

When they grew tired of listening, Unc' Billy whispered to Jimmy Skunk. Jimmy Skunk grinned, and then he crept a little way down the long hall and began to scratch with his stout claws, as if he were digging. When he stopped, Unc' Billy put his mouth down close to the doorway and barked as nearly like Reddy Fox as he could. Then Jimmy began to dig again, and pretty soon Unc' Billy barked again. Then all three

stole softly away and hid behind some bushes.

"Ah reckon Brer Rabbit is
right smart wide awake instead of
going to sleep fo' the winter!"
chuckled Unc' Billy.

XXVI

Peter Rabbit Learns His Lesson

PETER RABBIT, curled up in the little bedchamber at the end of the long hall in the old house made a long time ago by Grandfather Skunk, twisted and turned and tried to make himself feel sleepy. But the harder he tried, the more wide awake he seemed to feel. Then he began to think of Reddy and Granny Fox and what would happen if by any chance they should find him there fast asleep, and right while he was thinking about it, he heard a noise that made him jump so that he bumped his head.

Peter didn't think anything about the bump on his head! No, Sir, Peter didn't even notice it. He was too frightened. He held his breath and listened, while his heart went pit-a-pat, pit-a-pat. There it was again, that noise he had heard before! Someone was in the long, dark hall! There was no doubt about it. He could hear claws scratching. Whoever it was, was digging. Digging! The very thought made every hair on

[187]

Peter Rabbit stand on end. He knew that Johnny Chuck had gone to sleep for the winter. He knew that Jimmy Skunk could walk right in without any trouble, and that Jimmy never takes any trouble that he can avoid. He knew that Bobby Coon and Unc' Billy Possum don't go into houses underground unless they have to, to get away from danger, and very seldom then.

If someone was digging in the long, dark hall, it could mean but one thing — that it must be someone too big to get in without making the hall larger; and the only ones he could think of were

Bowser the Hound and Reddy and Granny Fox! Peter shivered and shook, for unlike Johnny Chuck's house, this one had no back door.

"If it's Bowser the Hound, he may get tired and go away. Anyway, I can soon tell, for he will sniff and snuff and blow the sand out of his nose," thought Peter, and strained his ears to hear the first sniff.

But there were no sniffs or snuffs. Instead, Peter heard a sound that made his heart almost stop beating again. It was a bark, a bark that sounded very much like the bark of Reddy Fox, and it came from just outside the door! That could mean but one thing — that Old Granny Fox was digging her way into the little bedchamber, while Reddy kept watch outside.

"Oh dear! Oh dear! Why wasn't I content to live as I always have lived? Whatever did I try to do something I never was intended to do for?" cried Peter to himself, and shook with fright harder than ever.

There was nothing to do but to sit still and wait. Peter sat as still as ever he could. After a little while, the noise in the long, dark hall stopped. Peter waited and waited, but all was still, and he began to feel better. Perhaps old Granny Fox didn't know that he was there at all, and had grown tired of digging and had gone away. Peter waited a long time and then peeped out into the long hall. Way up at the end he could see light where the door-way was, and by this he knew that no one was in the hall.

Little by little, his heart going pit-a-pat, Peter crept up until he could peep outside. No one was to be seen. With his heart almost in his mouth, Peter sprang out and started for the dear Old Briar-patch as fast as his long legs

[*191*]

could take him. And then he heard a sound that made him stop suddenly and sit up.

"Ha, ha, ha! Ho, ho, ho! Hee, hee, hee!"

There, behind some bushes, Unc' Billy Possum, Bobby Coon, and Jimmy Skunk were laughing fit to kill themselves.

Then Peter knew that they had played a joke on him, and he shook his fist at them. But down in his heart he was glad, for he knew that he had learned his lesson — that he had no business to try to do what Old Mother Nature had never intended that he should do.

[*192*]